ARTHURIAN THINGS
A Collection of Poems

Melissa Ridley Elmes

www.darkmythproductions.com/publications

Dark Myth Publications, a division of
The JayZoMon/Dark Myth Company.
21050 Little Beaver Rd, Apple Valley, CA 92308

ISBN: 978-1-652-48851-4

First Printing January 2020

Dark Myth Publications is a registered trademark of The JayZoMon/Dark Myth Company

10 9 8 7 6 5 4 3 2 1

Table of Contents

Table of Contents (Cont'd)

Table of Contents (Cont'd)

Dedications

For my family, near and far, born, chosen, and created

And all my fellow Arthurian enthusiasts

Acknowledgments

Like many nerds who didn't quite have a grasp on how to make their inner lives work in the outer world and spent far too much time and energy trying to fit in instead of embracing their weird while growing up, my life is more or less a mosaic of "right place, right time," "It seemed like a good idea at the time," "well, why not?" "what's the worst that can happen?" "I wonder what would happen if I …" and "If I could … I would … " tempered (in adulthood) with the ability to make the most of opportunities that present themselves, a strong work ethic once my attention is harnessed, an overactive imagination, good old-fashioned stubbornness, and not a little luck. I would therefore like to begin by thanking David K. Montoya, who contacted me out of the blue via Messenger to ask: "Hey, are you thinking about entering our *Open Contract Challenge*?" I hadn't been, until that moment, which turned out to be a turning point for me as a writer (and also gave me a great "how I spent my summer" anecdote this year.) Thanks as well to Molly Hamilton, former student, fellow writer, treasured friend, who recommended that I submit my poetry to *The World of Myth* magazine, thus rendering me eligible to enter the *Open Contract Challenge* for writers who had published in the magazine. These two seemingly benign and isolated incidents brought me into *The JayZoMon/Dark Myth Company*, where I've found so much opportunity to stretch my wings and roll around in creativity and invention.

I also want to thank my writing teachers in the Lindenwood University MFA in Writing program: Gillian Parrish, Eve Jones, Kali VanBaale, Anothai Kaewkaen, Andrew Pryor, Wm. Anthony Connolly, Tony D'Souza, and Nicole McInness. The lessons I learned from them individually and collectively are too legion to be listed here but can be boiled down to five truths: "You are a writer. You do not need permission to write. You do not have to explain why you write. You decide what you write. And you absolutely do need to take time to write." Thanks for re-training my intellectually-inclined mind to remember how to play with words, and for providing me with the opportunity to rediscover that writing and reading books are not just the tools of my career, but things inherent to who I am and how I make sense of myself and the worlds and communities I inhabit, and also the primary source of my intrinsic happiness. (Reader, if you're still reading this: *It's true that you know who you are when you are ten. Don't let the world beat it out of you.*)

Thanks to my Facebook friends, many (though by no means all!) of them fellow medievalists and Arthurian scholars and enthusiasts, who responded to my ninth-hour plea to "Give me the name of one THING—not any of the obvious ones, like Round Tables and shields and swords and thrones and Excalibur and rings and beds and tapestries and musical instruments and stones—just a quotidian, everyday THING—that could be present in a scene from an Arthurian story. Any (not obvious) thing (physical item)" when I was completely tapped out and could not think of another item to write into the collection; 67 responses later, I found the missing thing (and had a whole host of new ones to consider for future inventions!) I am so grateful for the community of friends, family, thinkers, writers, inventors, entrepreneurs, lawyers, librarians, fashionistas, athletes, artists, dancers, gamers, and just plain nerdy cool folks I've gathered over the years—my "web on the Web"—who play along with energy and enthusiasm, indulge my quirks and dark and twisty moments, and offer all the support, advice, encouragement, and fellowship I could wish for. Never underestimate the value of your tribe, even (and in today's world, maybe especially) your virtual one.

Finally, thanks to my husband Nick, and my daughters, Anna and Fallon, for bringing the joy. And also, for the Great Paradox of both giving me the time I need to write and refusing to allow me to write all the time. I count myself very lucky indeed to be among those writers in this world whose family fully supports my work, and even luckier to share my off hours with you. I love you 3000.

With gratitude,

Melle

Author's Foreword

I've been reading, and thinking, and teaching, and writing about the Arthurian legends for the better part of my adult life, and even after so much time with them I never cease to be surprised by the adaptive and expansive nature of these stories. No matter how familiar you might be with them there is always something new to discover in what has been told, and some bit left untold until someone finally tells it. Perhaps this seeming endlessness of it, how it expands to make room for an infinite variety of interpretations and interpolations (the original multiverse, if you will!) is one reason the legend of King Arthur and his Knights of the Round Table has been so popular with storytellers in every story medium humans have devised—prose, poetry, comic books, sculptures, paintings, stained-glass windows, tapestries, games, toys, television shows, movies, to name but a few. You would think we would reach a saturation point, but it seems neither storytellers nor audiences believe in such a thing as too much Arthuriana.

While most Arthurian stories and adaptations feature King Arthur and one or more of his usual companions—Queen Guinevere, Sir Lancelot, Sir Gawain, Sir Gareth, Sir Gaheris, Sir Bedivere, Sir Pellinore, Sir Tristan, King Mark, Queen Isolde, Sir Kay, Sir Bors (I could go on and name dozens more, but you get the idea) little attention is paid to their inner worlds—their thoughts and emotions— and even less attention is typically paid to the things of the Arthurian world, beyond the standard *Round Table, Sword Excalibur, Holy Grail* references. And so, recently, I have found my mind leaping into action, thinking about the everyday things and beings that of course must be there alongside the well-known elements, however unremarked. And from there, I have wondered: if these walls and halls and bedrooms and chambers and rings and cups and hills and meadows and lakes and rivers and weapons and beasts could talk, if they could tell the stories from their particular points-of-view, *what would they say?*

I haven't been able to shake the idea. As I've mused over it, I've thought: If Arthurian nonhumans tell their tales and we listen, could we gain more insight and different perspectives on these well-trod paths? Could we be surprised and astonished and find new joys and different concerns in these well-known characters? Could we be enchanted all over again by stories we think we know so well, stories that have been told a thousand times in a thousand different ways?

And then, I've thought: Isn't it about time we gave the things and beasts of the Arthurian world a chance to step into the limelight? After all, they have been there the whole time, waiting patiently for us to notice them. Waiting for the master narrative to make room for them. Waiting for someone to listen to and record their voices, adding them back into the world they already share. And while we're at it, how about some room for what the legendary characters think and feel, not just what they do and how?

And so, here are the stories we've heard a thousand times, told a thousand different ways—but not this way.

Not until now.

Melissa Ridley Elmes
2019

ARTHURIAN THINGS
A Collection of Poems

What the Kitchen-Cat Thought

Look—forgive me if this sounds cynical
but you people make such a big deal of it all—
Camelot, the most chivalric of communities,
Camelot, where King Arthur reigns supreme,
Camelot, home of the most valorous knights,
Camelot, where the most beautiful women reside,
Where dreams come true and fortunes are made—
yet for all that, the mice here are just mice
they taste the same as the mice where you live
and the same as mice taste anywhere else
(Or so I've noticed in the lives I've lived thus far)
and so, I can't
help but wonder
whether all this
wonder is not a
bit misplaced,
Whether Camelot
is not as ordinary
as its mice.

1

A Cut Rose in Guinevere's Chamber Meditates on Mortality

When that green-kirtled lady-in-waiting
plucked me away from my sisters I despaired
knowing it meant certain death
that I would never see my family again
and they would never know what became of me.
But, as I rested in the cut-crystal bowl where she placed me
with my life essence dripping out of my stem into the water
temporarily sustaining my life despite my death-wound,
I saw the Queen they call Guinevere and realized she, too
had been harvested from her family
and felt her life essence draining as she rested in this room,
far from all she knew and held dear,
plucked by King Arthur as I was plucked by the lady-in-waiting
(Which just goes to prove a king's no different than a servant:
when all's said and done, humans take what humans want.)
Maybe this is merely the fate of beautiful living things
in a world that loves them but cannot keep them
and maybe it's for the best, after all
that it was I who was plucked to join the queen
and wait for youth to pass away and surrender to the withering
of old age; my scent's the most lovely
my petals are the softest of all my family
and most pleasing to the eye and nose
and may they bring the queen some brief mortal joy
as she withers and dies alongside me
more slowly, but with no fewer sorrows and regrets
no lesser loneliness and longing.

2

What a Chicken Noticed About Sir Kay

Nobody likes Sir Kay
He is a churl, they say
Unrefined, uncouth, prone
To saying cruel and nasty things
To angry outbursts, to disdain
For the queen and, really
Essentially everyone—
But could you see the tears
In his eyes as he wrings the necks
Of the chickens that go into the pies
You might understand his outer prickly
To be protection for his inner soft—
Like feathers protecting the skin
Waiting to be plucked away,
To reveal the gentle, malleable parts
Hidden from view by nature—
Let me tell you, I know one day
It will be my turn to be baked in a pie
And I hope Sir Kay is the one
To wring my neck and pluck my feathers
And lay me bare to the world.
No other knight would shed a tear
No other knight would see me so truly
No other knight would be as humane
(Even if he complains bitterly,
swears up a storm the whole time.)

3

The Rain Explains Something About Arthurian Tournaments

Maybe it's not obvious, but while you watch these men-at-arms
Bear in mind that chivalry has its limits as well as its charms.

I won't disclose who, but know this:
more than one of those renowned knights
prays for rain every tournament day
to avoid another unnecessary fight.

Mother Moon Beams Down on Her Favorite

You probably never imagined
The moon might have a favorite face
To illuminate with her beams all the night long
(It's true that mothers don't often admit
A preference for one child over the others.)
But if I'm honest, it's Galahad's forehead
I love best of all to caress—
So pale and so pure.

A Sheep Sets Things Straight Concerning Castle-Field Relations

You might not think sheep in a field
Could have any insight into what goes on
In Camelot, so far removed are we
From its inner workings, until we are
Transformed by the alchemy of cookery
Into lamb and roast mutton, to be
Eaten and absorbed into the lords and ladies
At some everyday meal or grand feast.

But a castle is not a quiet place
And secrets are not safe there, and nor
Are there private spaces with no prying eyes
or human tongues to tell of what goes on.

So sometimes, a knight will wander among us
Whispering a secret he must tell and keep at once
Into our sheep's ears, and we *baa-aa* our promise
Never to reveal what he has dared to share.

And sometimes a couple, he fair and she lovely
Will come to see the new little lambs
And then drift off into a field's corner
For an afternoon's dalliance, knowing
lamb's bleats are as good as an oath to secrecy
And that no one will imagine they'd be here

Among next month's lunches and dinners,
Next year's woolen cloaks and tunics.

The Wishing Well Wishes

Just once, I wish one of those knights
or ladies, or their servants, or, really
anyone from Camelot, that
kingdom high upon the hill
(Where supposedly everything and
everyone is perfect and without peer
and yet so many flee to my side
asking for all they can't buy or sell)
Would come to visit *me*, just to see
a well-crafted well, instead of begging
for things we all know I can't give.

The Wishing Well Dishes

They might surprise you, the wishes they make.
I mean, not all of them are unexpected—
Pellinore always wishes to catch his questing beast
And Guinevere of course comes twice a month
Tossing her pennies in hopes this time, they'll take
And Lancelot will be hers without treason.
But Lancelot, ah, he does not wish for Guinevere
But for Arthur's forgiveness, and also
The chance to return home and not in disgrace
To watch the sun set across the lake beside
His ancestral home once more.
Palamedes has asked variously for glory
And a new steed, and a better room
(Apparently, they put him up in the high North Tower
And it's chilly and damp and he's last on the servants'
Progress to light the evening fires in this cold clime.)
Gareth often wishes for a room of his own
Because Gaheris snores and Gawain is loud
When he comes roaring in at drunk o'clock.
Gawain came once, and wished on a ha'penny
For a parrot that can talk, like the one he saw
Once long ago as a child, before knighthood
Stripped him of the ability to enjoy such wonders.
Some knights wish for wealth, some for women
Some wish for a dog, or a falcon, or a kitten

Some wish for better arms, some for better skills
Some for nicer clothing, some for fewer drills
Other knights wish for trifles, really—
And Arthur, their king?
Arthur sits beside me, alone and pensive
Queries whether I or any other thing can know
The hardships of mortal men who reign
Bemoans the treacheries all around him
Laments the inevitable imminent failure
Of the great experiment he's sought to perform
—And wishes he had never been born.

A Sword in the Armory

In truth, I'd rather I'd been melted down and then
tempered and hammered into four horseshoes—

Far nobler to protect the feet of gentle beasts
than hack down yet another hapless youth.

But being iron, no one bothered asking me
What I would like to be when I grew up.

The Questing Beast Joins #MeToo

Sir Pellinore has been chasing me for years.

Sure, it's a dashing tale of adventure, and of course
You've always rooted for him to catch his beast.

Have you never wondered what *I* thought of it all?

If I wanted to be pursued, if I was asking for it
Don't you think I'd have let him catch me by now?

I am not flattered and he is not dedicated.

He's just another man who refuses to believe
Everything and everyone won't simply be his.

His passion is my torment, and let me also add:

There are a lot of beasts and beings in these tales
With the same problem—these "men being men."

Just because he's a knight doesn't make it all right.

A Sheet's Analysis of What Goes on Between the Sheets

It really is nothing to me
if you want to toss me over
a balcony, display me for
the masses to judge, to see
the blood of women's privacy
and call them "whore" and "slut" and such—

But consider as well that not everything
on sheets is so readily visible; this practice
is classic confirmation bias writ large
and you know as well as I its purpose:
to remind onlookers that women's truths
don't matter all that much—

Their tears of grief and humiliation
their heartbreaks and devastations
the seed of the men spilled on the sheets
of the women they choose who are not their wives
these secrets, too, sheets keep
and might reveal, if you bothered to look past the blood—

If it were about more than just the stains
of men's honor and of women's shame.

The Great Hall

At the heart of any kingdom rests a Great Hall large and grand,
appointed per the royal custom in each new reign, fashioned
with those luxuries deemed most pleasing by the king and queen
and those whose graces render their opinions most important
whenever possible irrespective of cost or of difficulty to obtain,
so to demonstrate to all and sundry each king's largesse, his
wealth beyond measure, and why his rule is worthy of memory.
Well and truly, humans can't remember them all, but the Hall
does; my walls have seen kings and their things come and go,
serve as a cultural reliquary, museum of many meals partaken

and more: of speeches, disputes & discussions, of the fates
of kingdoms lying in the balance over appetizers but secured
by dessert; of diplomats idling over drinks at a dinner's end,
hoping to gain the king's favor for their lords; of dalliances,
dreams, and blossoming loves; of relationships torn asunder;
of centuries of songs sung by bards and scops; of dancing
and merriment and games through the generations; of all the
social mores, the ways and means of a given society through
out its many iterations; finally, these walls tell their own stories
scarred by weapons wielded by enemies, covered over with

tapestries, the finest and costliest wrought by human hands
a record of death and destruction lying just beneath their cloth
surfaces for anyone who peeks beneath to remark upon, stark

warnings that wherever men gather together they are but one
point of pride from downfall, one argument away from sudden
severing of alliances. Don't dwell on those faded battle scars,
the scratches in the stonework showing when last this place,
its community, faced destruction; that was then and is not now,
at least for now. Look instead at my wonderful wove wall-rugs,
so large and lush, with their scenes of ancient landscapes and

beautiful people, of heroic warriors at the height of their glory,
so finely wrought that they seem to breathe, eager to speak,
to share their songs and stories. Shot through with spun gold
These priceless draperies beckon the eye to linger in amaze
ment, it is hard to tear away your gaze to look upon the room
they clothe and cloak; yet, that room, sumptuously appointed,
here the subject of your attention, is well worth the looking:
Long, wide trestle-tables line both sides of my center aisle,
on which is rolled out a carpet richly embroidered, linking door
to dais. A hundred candles light your way, the fire in the grate

warms body and spirits in equal measure, thus I offer comfort.
White linens soft and well-pressed so that no crease or fold
disturbs their broad expanse drape across my tables, anchored
by bowls and cups of finest bone china, by centerpieces only
imaginable by the wildest of fancies, beckoning to every eye:
Riots of birds and flowers, vines and otherworldly mechanical
things designed to delight and amaze their onlooker once
set into motion at some predetermined point in the evening,
a wave of continuous stimulation of all of the senses, and in
the end that is what a feast is for; my role as Great Hall that

of host to a host of humans whose faculties long for astonishing
things beyond the ordinary and beyond their ken. I am the hall
you've heard of, I am that place of wonder. As you wander in

you face the high dais, where king and queen and their most honored guests and treasured companions occupy their time with fine foods, rich wines, glad revelry, gay music; My dais is hung all about with silken banners, a canopy of tapestries, handi work of masters without peer, embroidered and embellished, across these weavings are scattered peerless gems of priceless quality, gleaming in the firelight and framing this lovely tableau.

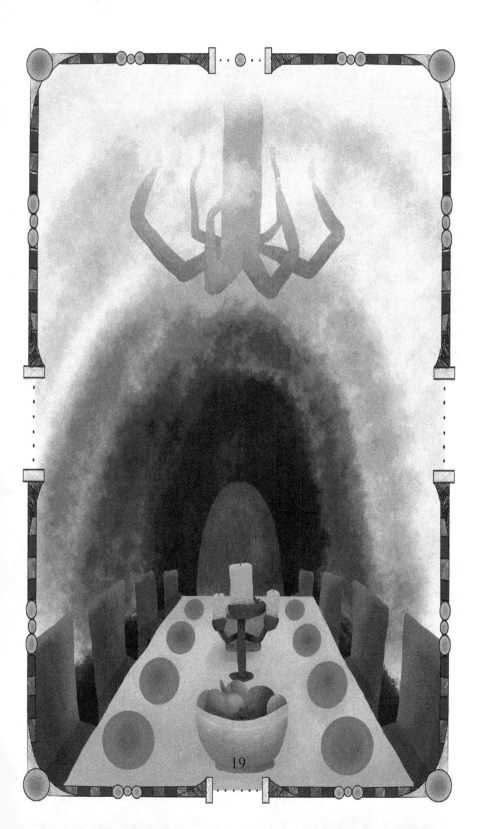

A Lyre Begs a Commission

I tire of singing the noble deeds
The tragic downfalls of great knights
The treacheries of Morgan le Fay
The sorrows of Queen Guinevere

Play on me instead a ditty, a song
of the people, for the people, let me
laugh aloud, find joy in my work!

Surely those noble knights know
one bawdy lyric, one hale chorus
to belt along with gusto in this hall!

Let's put limericks to music and
wink at their meaning, glad contrast
to battle hymns and sobbing ballads.

Pass the ale, strum my strings,
let me spring into lively tune
tonight by the light of the moon
and don't sit listening quietly—!

You come and sing and dance with me.

The Lyre's Limericks, I

There once was a *Lancelot du Lac*
renowned both for charm and attack.
Brought to court by the Queen
he soon found himself 'tween
love and duty, alas and alack!

Of *Sir Gawain of Orkney* 'tis said
he is ruled by his heart, not his head—
Yet when Bertilak's Lady
was acting real shady
Young Gawain tried to hide in his bed!

You lot ought to harken to *Sir Kay*
as he mutters to himself all the day
traipsing through the castle
serving as seneschal
and critiquing your uncourtly ways!

The Rosary of the Hermit in the Wood Reminds You of the Importance of Faith and Hope in Stories

The hermit in the wood prays as Camelot crumbles
Counting on me the hours, days, weeks, months
Years, an eternity

A litany of faith
A litany of hope
A litany to remember, preserve what he can
Of a storybook world that is vanishing into human error

Yet again; every time you humans think you are better
Than you were, you screw it up; hermits know this.

Don't say he's wasting his time
Don't say actions speak louder than words
Don't say that saying a rosary is a fool's errand
Or that faith is the opiate of the masses

(Criticize religion all you like.
It is not religion that matters; hermits know this.)

But do not criticize the faith and hope of anyone
Much less those who rely on them as the foundation
Of stories they hold dearest; press them into service

Of the present, the future, of dreams, of desires

Faith and hope are not the servants of religion
But of the human condition; hermits know this.

Who among you has the right to criticize belief in unseen things?
To criticize this hermit counting beads on a rosary in the face
Of the end of everything else he has been led to believe in?
Are some stories more valuable than others? No. No. No.

Faith and hope belong to everyone, and in every story
Humans tell, they play a part; hermits know this.

Sometimes faith and hope are the only path forward
And as kingdoms fall and dreams fade into grim reality
It's faith and hope that carry the stories forward
Tales told at bedtime to fuel children's dreams

If Camelot is to survive, rise again
It will be in children's tales
And children's tales are wove
Of faith and hope.

It's my job to help the hermit count his way
Back from fear and despair, back into what he knows.

Come, join the hermit
Count each bead into a story
And let me help you, too.

The Pigeon on the Parapet

From up here Arthur's knights look fine:
Noble, chivalrous, ready to wage battle
with his enemies, keep his name burnished
in the books you so love to read, put their
bodies on the line again (armor's grand
until you find yourself in hand-to-hand
combat, falling in mud, in blood
slipping on somebody else's insides,
drowning in a puddle on a field
where you were knocked over face-first
by a horse, piled three and four men deep.)
Yes, from this bird's-eye view
Arthur's knights are bright in the sun,
their chainmail shines untested, untried.
You can't see them shaking with fear.
You can't hear them begging their ladies
for *just one kiss, just one*
as they march off once more into
someone else's pride-driven war.

The Throne's Thoughts

Men court me and what I represent;
go to great lengths to establish my importance, and hence
their importance when they are seated upon me.

Perverse to take pride in something so fleeting and untenable.
Perverse to believe in my permanence, when I am man-made
and thus, inherently destructible.

A Ring in the Treasury Summarizes the Basic Arthurian Tale Plot

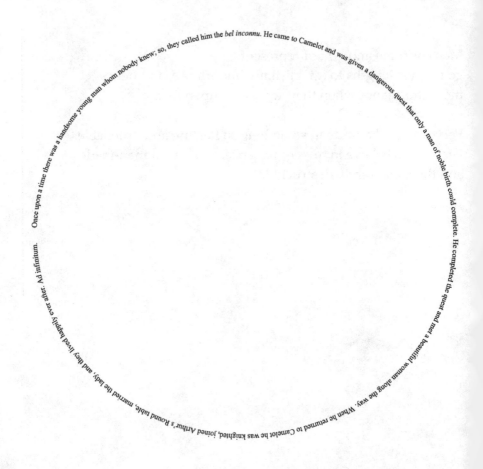

Once upon a time there was a handsome young man whom nobody knew; so, they called him the *bel inconnu*. He came to Camelot and was given a dangerous quest that only a man of noble birth could complete. He completed the quest and met a beautiful woman along the way. When he returned to Camelot he was knighted, joined Arthur's Round table, married the lady; and they lived happily ever after. Ad infinitum.

Gawain's Shield Admires Her Pentagram Tattoo

I have been by his side, constant companion, throughout
his adventures; seen him at his best and his worst, stayed

true and solid in his grip in joust, in battle, always with my
five-sided pentagram tattoo facing the world, record of his

excellences: five keen senses; five dexterous fingers; five
virtues: fellowship, generosity, chastity, charity, courtesy;

devotion to the five joys of Mary in Christ, and Christ's
five wounds; truly say I he boasts no mortal peer, and

only I am Gawain's equal among things that outlast men,
share his virtues, openly and indelibly carved into my side.

The Door to Guinevere's Bedchamber Resigns

I thought doors were built for privacy,
to close out the world, contain secrets
offer security and protection,
A haven from the world beyond —
and that's a noble occupation,
the job I was proud to take on
for Camelot's comely Queen.

I've remained closed and bolted.
I've slammed properly to indicate
her rage as needed, and I've shut
softly, not a peep, in early and late
hours according to her will.
I've locked and unlocked only for her,
dedicated my career loyally to her care.

But with time I've wondered
as the tales-told run rampant
despite my excellent job performance,
years guarding the queen's sanctuary:
why have doors at all
when everyone is so certain they know
what transpires behind them when shut?

I've come to believe men want the door closed

28

so they can invent for themselves
what happens behind it—a sort of writer's prompt
for the next wild tale, the next juicy secret,
the next kingdom-destroying rumour—
That maybe doors here are employed for a reason
I hadn't imagined: to manufacture treason.

Well, if that's the case, I quit—you folk
get something else to do your dirty work.

A Goose Feather Quill Refuses to Spill Secrets

I suppose you want me to spill
the secrets that I've learned
words drawn with gall ink
from my hollow stem
by humans holding me hostage
to communicate their desires
their hopes and dreams,
their plots and plans,
their loves and treasons.

I may be bent to human use
but I am still of the wing of the goose
and I claim my right to merely sigh
in the wind, as on the wing,
content to flourish, to swish silent
unless you can squeeze those few
remaining drops of ink from my
deepest recesses, and even then
those drops of ink can't share
what I know; the memory of the
hand that held me, the tracing
of my tip upon the parchment.

Humans may speak, may write,
spill their secrets, and ink may

assist them in these endeavors.
but while I have no choice but
to play accomplice in the moment,
I am mute ever after; you'll get no
more secrets out of me, unless
you dip me into an inkwell
and write out your own.

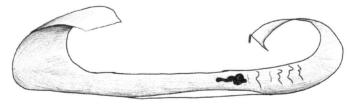

The Cat with her Basket of Kittens in the Scullery I

I am the only queen in Camelot ever to give birth.
You may decide for yourself whether
that's grounds for
tragedy or mirth.

The Cat with her Basket of Kittens in the Scullery II

Men measure men by many means—

by deeds of arms, how many others
they can topple off a horse, how many
others they can run through with sharp
objects;

by how many women they've wooed,
hugged, kissed, groped, fondled, fucked,
loved, left, knocked up, beaten into sub
mission;

by various accomplishments beyond
battle and bed: their ability to sing, to
dance, to play an instrument, to write
poems;

by how well they ride astride a horse,
how well they hunt and skin their prey
how far they travel any given day on
their quests;

In truth, the measure of a man may be had
by far simpler means—just come to this
scullery and see how gently he handles

my kits—

A man who can look on an innocent kitten
and not involuntarily reach to cuddle, not
visibly soften into gentle kindness, that is
no man,

but a monster. Perhaps the King, that great
King Arthur, instead of having all his knights
try to pull a sword from a stone to prove
their worth,

ought to have them pull a kit from this basket,
instead.

A Golden Ingot Contemplates its Unrealized Potential in the Treasury at Camelot

I could be a torc, a necklace, a bracelet or a ring—
Some maid's lovely thing.

I could be a shower of coins, a stack of pennies—
Some lord's spending-sprees.

I could be the pommel of a bright broadsword—
Some brave knight's reward.

I could be a golden-gleaming new king's crown—
Prince Arthur's renown.

I could be useful or gorgeous, melted down
and reformed, in town.

But I lie a block in this treasury, gathering dust—
My own dream's bust.

Such is the fate of many, many a collected thing
belonging to the king—

We rest inert, awaiting a moment when we matter
enough to share his world.

Arthurian Flies Request Unionization

We are the cast of thousands—
Nameless, faceless, unidentified, unremarked, unwritten—
Yet in every Camelot scene.

We are on the battlefields.
We are on the jousting fields.
We are in the stables.
We are in the woods.
We are by the waters.
We are in the meadows.
We are in the sculleries; and yes,
We hum in all the halls and bedchambers.

There is no place in the world where we are not.
We are so present that we are invisible to you,
Not-there on every page and in every image,
And here are just a few examples of our work:

[1]

We fly around the horses on hot days
Allowing them to toss their heads at us
You ooh and aah at their majestic beauty
The lush fullness of their swish-swish tails:
You ignore our presence.

[2]

We buzz throughout the battles
Overlooked and underheard
As the steel swords clang and
The men cry out in rage, pain, fear, death:
You ignore our presence.

[3]

We enter the hall through the same window
As the sparrow you can't help but remark on;
As a knight raises his glass for a toast one of us
Alights on the rim, is impatiently swiped away:
You ignore our presence.

[4]

We fly into the mouth of a mounted knight mid-charge
Causing him to gasp and choke, heightening
The drama of a jousting scene as you wonder
Will he fall from his steed and forfeit?
You ignore our presence.

[5]

We enter bedchambers before dark
wafting in through the open windows
Alighting on the bedframes; we might spy
Might fly back to share what we've seen—
But you ignore our presence.

We are swatted at by knights.
We are waved off by ladies.
We are blown at by horses.
We are slapped at by maids.
We are batted at by cats.
We are stabbed at by daggers.
We are flicked at by whips.
We are flattened by books.

And do you ever stop to notice?
Do you ever think: *what about the flies?*
Admit it: No, you do not.
You've never wondered about Arthurian flies.
We're just there. Like all the other things
Without names or specific roles. Window dressing
(especially after being smacked dead on a window.)

Look—
We're not asking for a spot at the Table
Or for a Round Table of our own.
We know we're not kings or knights
Or damsels-in-distress, or even
Fancy weapons or magical objects.
We're aware that in the grand scheme
We hardly factor, and we accept that.
But just about everyone around here
Gets to be seen at least once—
the kings and knights get names,
the swords and horses get names,
The castles and lakes get names,
Even the woods get names,
And most of the ladies as well.
Is it really that much to ask,

To see and name a fly or two,
Maybe even give one a story?

It's a thankless and dangerous job,
Being a fly in King Arthur's court.
And we're tired of the silent treatment.
It's about time we had our due.

Here are our demands: a union
That fights for our rights.
We want names and lines.
We want a featured scene, and
Eventually, a series of our own
In this medieval multiverse.

Arthurian Ants Join the Unionization Effort

We, too, are Arthuriana ...

We march into and out of the halls
right alongside those knights.
We join the flies as the nameless
and faceless nonhuman horde
on those battlefields; and more:
We are trampled and stomped
by feet, smooshed by fingers
and you've never noticed us,
Not Once. And that's really a pity
because if anyone had paid heed
to us as we marched to and fro
in the pantry, with our crumbs,
they might have noticed that
many of our number lay dead
around the apples, poisoned on
the job, and Sir Patryse might
still be alive to be killed on a
tournament or battlefield instead.
Many of us shared his ignominious
end, poisoned, enduring the malice
of one of those treacherous knights.
And so our job is as deadly as the
knights', the flies', and we, too,

would seek unionization, represen-
tation, to be granted our moment
in the spotlight, have paid our dues.

Arthurian Bees Weigh in on the Question of Unionization

We are a material collective.

Our products enrich their
Lives; they take our wax,
Our comb, our honey, they
Leave us nothing in return
But the occasional mass
Termination of our hives.

And yet, they value most
The mead which without us
Is impossible to create, and
The flowers we pollinate.

So yes, by all means, let's
Stand our ground, demand
A place at the table, force
A more equitable partnering
From our human counterparts.

Perhaps not merely a union,
But a golden guild is in order,
Generative and generous, and
No longer free and uncredited.

The Lyre and a Harp Compose a Jumping-Rope Ditty for Arthurian Dude-Bros

Dame Berti—*lak, lak, lak*
Was in the *sack, sack, sack*
With a robe of *silk, silk silk*
Shrugged off her *back, back, back*

She asked Ga*wain, wain, wain*
For just one *kiss, kiss, kiss*
He tried to *hide, hide, hide*
From that bold *Miss, Miss, Miss*

She pressed her *suit, suit, suit*
Tried to knock *boots, boots, boots*
Sir Gawain *refused, used, used*
Ain't that a *hoot, hoot hoot?*

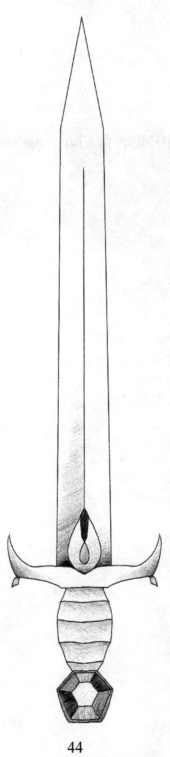

44

What a Poet Writes of Excalibur

Skin-slicer, organ-spiller
Burnished bright blade of
The Once and Future King—

Battle-rich instrument, sing, sing
The victories of Arthur,
King of the Britons—

Cut deep and true
through hides of England's enemies
spilling forth legends—

Then slip, sharp-tipped
into the lake waters of Avalon
and wait, wondrous weapon—

Romance will lose luster
And war will out
And iron swords shall sing again.

Excalibur Deals with Imposter Syndrome

It's hard, you know
Having the Big Name
The one everyone
Recognizes right away.

There are Expectations
When you're the one
They've all heard of,
The name they know.

The truth is, there are
More important swords
In King Arthur's life, but
I have a better publicist.

And yes, I'm feeling
Quite a lot of guilt
And not a little bit
Of Imposter Syndrome.

My therapist thinks it
Would be best if I
Came clean, owned up
To my limitations, so

Look, for the last time,
I'm NOT the sword in
the stone, not the one that
gave Arthur the throne.

And I DON'T have the
Magic powers, that would
Be my scabbard, and yes,
It's unfair she gets second

Billing and isn't ever named
In the credits, but in my
Defense I don't make
The rules and it wasn't

My choice to be the
Famous one, frankly
I hate the pressure and
Would prefer to just

Sit in the armory and
Be in a scene or two
As an extra, rather than
Always girded to Arthur

Always seen, never heard
Always discussed, never
Understood, always loved
But never for myself.

Also, for the record,
my real name is
Caledfwlch, but my

Publicist thought that
Was too hard to say.
Wow, that felt good,
Thanks for coming
To my Ted Talk.

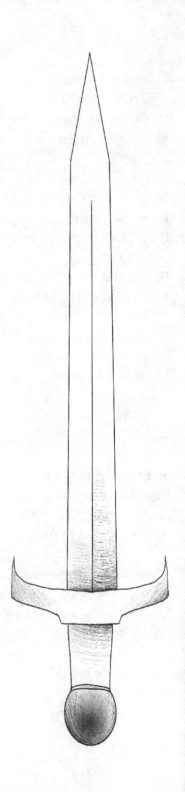

The Poisoned Apple's Unrecorded Testimony

Oh sure, at the Queen's gone-deadly feast
everyone falls to pieces over Sir Patryse—
"Help! Help! He's been poisoned! He's dead!
It's all Guinevere's fault, let's have her head!"

First of all, let's recall, that I am a victim, too—
Not only poisoned, but bitten into, and left to
roll to a lonely spot beneath the table, where
no one remembers or cares that I am even there.

If anyone bothered to pick me up, to ask me
    what I saw, I could have cleared things easily.
    Why of course Guinevere did not do it, I'd say,
        'Twas Sir Pyonell did the deed, and by the way

He spoke a monologue all the while, as he
    contrived to create a dread weapon of me,
        muttering and trying not to make a clatter,
        and here's what he had to say about the matter:

Sir Gawain is known to love fruit of all kinds.
When he reaches for this basket he'll find
this lovely apple irresistible, he'll take it, eat,
and thus by my poison be swept off his feet!

Not love, but hate, will fuel this feet-sweeping.
and all his kinsmen will find themselves weeping,
    and that's justice for my kinsman Lamorak
        whom Gawain killed; it's thus I'll pay him back!

And there you have it, that's what occurred
the idea 'twas Guinevere's doing is absurd!
But you'll never know, having left me to rot
Poisoned, bitten, dropped and forgot, in
Camelot.

49

The Lyre's Limericks II

Oh, a knight's always after a quest
Always wants to be put to the test
Unless it's for love —
Then, dear God above!
All he wants is an easy conquest!

To the ladies, I just have to say:
Why throw all your freedoms away?
Don't marry a knight —
You'll lose him to fight!
Just flirt with him all through the day!

All may be fair in love and war —
But war's deadly, and death is a bore
Choosing love instead
You're sound in the head
And sure to enjoy your life more!

The Round Table Doesn't Get It

I was de
signed to ne
ver actu
ally be
full, to al
ways have room
for the next
knight who comes
along, and
if I can
enact ne
verending
hospital
ity, and hu
mans made me,
why can't you
humans just
do it too?

Arthurian Porn

Lusty Ladies
Frisky Fairies
Horny Hermits
Moaning Maidens
Kissing Kings
Quivering Queens
Fornicating Friars
Erotic Elves
Gasping Giants
Wanton Witches
Writhing Wizards
Naughty Nuns
Saucy Servants
Lancing Lords
Kneading Knights
Sexy Squires
Pricking Pages
Stroking Sages

—Was it good for you?

A Rat's Perspective

I'truth, I know none of those knights' names
Nor anything any of them has done.

And i'truth, none of them has ever noticed me, either —
Or I'd most likely be dead:

Spitted on a sword
Squashed underfoot
Splatted against a wall
Shaken into rigor mortis

My head crushed
My tail cut off
My back broken
My eye shot out

So i'truth, no, I know none of those knights' names —
And I really don't care to.

The Wall Around the Castle Has No Idea What It's Actually For

Been here a hundred years and more

Built before anyone's living memory

Still not sure what my job is

Keep who out?

Keep who in?

Whose Camelot?

Who is Camelot?

Who is not?

Am I protection? Am I fortification?

Do I say "Keep out!" or "Stay, you are safe here?"

At least I look strong and mighty

Imposing and impenetrable

(If also a little the worse for wear here and there)

Pretty all draped with ivy

Like something out of a story

Towering over a castle

Full of knights and ladies

Signifying anything and nothing all at once

Defined and redefined

Purposed and repurposed

Hairs in a Horn Comb

What do you make of a few stray hairs,
lovely long and red-gold snarls, twisted in the tines of a
horn comb?

If you are the maiden who shed those hairs,
you may count them, anxious, wondering if your mane
has thinned.

If you are the maidservant, you may pluck
the hairs from the comb, impatient, toss them away into
the fire.

But if you are Lancelot, and the hairs, Guinevere's,
you collect them, reverent, braid them into a soft, bright
love's ring,

wear them close to your heart as a precious thing.
And if you are another, indifferent knight? You never notice
they're there.

Heroic Hygiene (What a Pocket Knife Knows)

Galahad and Perceval
are supposedly the pinnacle
of Arthurian success.
But even Grail knights
aren't perfect—

Galahad uses me
to trim his nails
and drops the filings
behind a bench in the Great Hall—
A fine thing for the maids to find!

Then, Perceval borrows me,
scrapes the dirt and blood
from under his fingertips
and wipes them under his chair
at the Round Table.

And don't get me started
on what they do with me
where blisters are involved—
even I don't like to think
too much about that.

Web-Weavers (A Spider's Meditation)

Why do the ladies compliment one another on the beauty of their laces
the intricacies of their crocheting, the handiwork of their tatting, then
wave away my morning's work with disdainful hands, as though it does
not rival theirs in every way?

But I supposed I should not wonder too much at such behaviors; after
all, they are kind to each other when the moods strikes, when they
are in good graces with one another, but it all goes rather quickly sour
when one seems better than the rest.

Their jealousies and pettinesses do not permit them to truly admire that
which is admirable; their admiring is coveting when all's said and done:
either they want the other's creation, or the other's craft. And there's my
answer, then: they know they can't have mine.

We all weave webs, but mine are nature-born, not borne of someone's
teaching and someone's training, not taught but remembered from
some well of instinct they can never know or harness, and their webs
are spun of spite and frustration.

I am the happier weaver, the weaver with a purpose beyond mere
efforts to pass the time and garner praise and acclaim; I weave
for myself alone, not to please others or to put them in their places
like the webs wove by those women.

And I suppose, then, they must destroy my creations whenever they
see them, unwitting reminders of their limitations and their longings,
the things they want and can't have, want to be and can't be—and who
would believe they could wish to be weavers like me?

Hey, Nonny Nonny (Another Lyre's Ditty)

Oh, the men of Camelot are bold
And the women all so bonny
Yes, everyone's worthy of a tune—
Sing Hey! Nonny, nonny.

Now Camelot's a lovely place
A castle large and luxurious
Yes, a fortress worthy of a tune—
Sing, Hey! Nonny, nonny.

And the king of Camelot's a lord
The likes of who's not been seen before
Yes, he's a king worthy of a tune—
Sing Hey! Nonny, nonny.

And every knight's in his own right
A man of great derring-do
Yes, each knight's worthy of a tune—
Sing Hey! Nonny, nonny.

And the queen of Camelot's a lady
Whose beauty is far beyond peer
Yes, worthy of a tune's our Guinevere—
Sing Hey! Nonny, nonny.

So come one, come all, come dance along
Come listen to this lively song
Of a place and people worthy of a tune—
Sing Hey! Nonny, nonny.

The Skipping Stone's Adventure

My story starts on an ordinary day as many stories do.
I was by the shore of the shining-watered lake, a stone
Among many stones, caught the eye of a knight's page
Having a day off; he gathered me up, rubbed my sides
And exclaimed, "this one, yes, is perfect!" and put me
Into a pocket where I scarce had time to take stock of
My situation before I was pulled out again. That page
Next pulled me out and palmed me, again remarking
Upon my remarkable quality, the smoothness and heft
Of me; and then without warning, he tossed me away.

I *skip—skip—skip—skipped* across the smooth surface
Of the lake and then began my descent; at first the sun
Light lit the way, first clear golden, then tinged bluish
Green, then deepening into warm watery blue-green,
Then slowly browning as the sun abandoned me to my
Dive down to the depths and all grew dark. At first, I
Was enjoying my adventure; rocks rarely get to see
Much of the world after all and I thought I might have
A story to tell, when all's said and done—after all, I
Had been selected by the page, called the Chosen One.

But as I dove lower, lower still into the murky depths
I realized that the page had made choices for me that
I might not be quite okay with; did I *want* to leave

The shores of the lake, the warm sun and gentle rain
The company of all my kith and kin and everything
I'd ever known to go on this adventure? Whether I did
Or whether I did not, did not matter now; I was on my
Way. And where to? Could I swim? Could I survive?
What if land rocks aren't so suited for watery climes?
In truth, being chosen wasn't all you might hope for.

I began to worry and to fret as the water went so dark
I couldn't see anything; to wonder whether it would
Hurt when I hit the bottom and if I would survive this
Fall, and where I would wind up since I had no control
Over my descent, no agency in my actions. Carried by
The current I could feel I drifted side-to-side and some
Times a bit more to the right and then a lot to the left,
And then I began to feel myself rubbing against things
That did not feel like anything I'd come into contact
With on land: things cool and slick and slimy and scaly.

This might have been terrifying in deep-dark water
Where nothing can be seen, except that to my utter
Surprise the light around me changed again not back
To sunshine but some otherworldly gleam in which
Could be seen my new surroundings: I saw so many
Things for which I did not yet have names but I can
Tell them now: milfoil and seaweed and hydrilla and
Algae and fish, so many fish, small and silvery and
Darting among the plants, an underwater garden so
Strange and lovely I would have gasped if rocks did.

And I forgot to be afraid as I took it all in and saw
The beauty of the deep, this waterworld into which
I had been sent by a boy who would never himself

Make the journey, never see these things well worth
The seeing. I was a shoreline rock out of place but
Truly I tell you in that moment as those things came
shimmering into view in the unsourced gloom-glow
I saw that stranger in this strange land though I was
So out of place in this slick, smooth, silken watery
Landscape, yet I could settle here without sorrowing.

I became weightier as I went deeper, felt the water
Moving with me, almost like the caress of fingers
On my surface and then with a tiny *plip* I reached
The bottom of the lake, nestled into silken sand and
Had the chance to take stock of my fate. To my left
Was a grove of naiad, moving rainbows and silver
Ribbons threading through the soft green as fish did
What it is that fish do so far from the eyes of land.
I have never seen such a living place, where nothing
Lies still, not even the rocks, not even me. I drifted.

I had never before known what it is to move without
Some other being's touch—a foot's kick, a hand's
Grasp, a paw or hoof sending me skittering; the flow
Of the current was a revelation, carrying me through
This place like a path that moved by magic means so
Gently I scarcely felt the motion at all, and would be
Hard-pressed to describe it, save that I was in one
Place and then, hours later, in quite another, and who
Knew the lake was so vast below the surface? I might
Roam for years and not see all its nooks and crannies.

As I traveled with the current, I began to see things
Men would recognize: men would do many deeds
heroic and ignoble if they knew what I know, if they

Saw the silver that was not fish, the gold scattered
Along the lake floor, centuries of penny-a-wishes
the rings and bracelets many a maid had tossed in
To test their lords: *Dive, find it if you love me!* And
More, so much more; men are careless with their
Objects and sometimes those things treasured most
Are lost along the way in ways no man can explain.

I cannot say how long I journeyed with the current
Along the lake bottom, or how many sights I saw
That filled me with wonder and delight before the
Moment when I rolled gently against something
That went clink! when I touched it; there, I saw a
Sword, long and gleaming, sharp as shark's fins
And on its hilt was writ all about: *I am Excalibur*
He who wields me shall be Once and Future King —
And that must be called the end of this adventure,
For what more could one stone hope to encounter?

The Grail

Humans argue over my true nature,
What I am understood to symbolize:

Am I the chalice of Christ's Last Supper
The Holy Grail of healing, vessel of
Eternal life?

Am I the cauldron of
The Goddess, appropriated by a
Patriarchy wholly out of step with
The Divine Feminine Truth?

But am I not in the end, if nothing else,
a cup made by a man, fashioned of clay,
Fired into service,

And am I any less an instrument
Of life everlasting and nurturing love
If all I do is quench the thirst of one
Parched pilgrim?

Things Thought in Passing: A Sonnet Cycle

I

Kay

I wish I knew just what it is about
me makes them so disdainful; am I not
brother to the king, Arthur's loyal lout?
And still for all my connections, I'm shut
out of the running for quests, for contests,
for every thing that makes a knight a knight,
and while our comrades fight over who's best
I'm left alone to ruminate my plight:
"*Sir Kay*," indeed, as though mere titles may
grant me the honored place that I deserve.
Truly I ask: who are any of *them*,
save men of courage and brawn and sheer nerve?
When we were boys, Arthur looked up to me.
I am so much more to him than they can see.

II

Tristan

I am renowned for music and for venery,
and known throughout this land for so much more;
and yet, I find myself reduced to beggary,
for life at court can only be heartsore.
I fell in love with Isolde, lady fair,
and she with me, but not by our own choice:
'twas a potion led us to it, though I swear
even without that potion, her sweet voice
would capture my sad soul with its dear sound;
her figure and her face entrap my heart
as strongly as that potion that we found.
Hence I did flee from court and we did part—
for I could not bear to be treason's source,
so I must keep miles 'tween self and remorse.

III

Isolde

I am a woman caught between two men,
and well I know the blame's assigned to me,
despite that I'm as much victim as them,
trapped once by magic; twice by king's decree.
Yet, outside eyes will see me as the bane
of knight and king, alike, source of their woes,
and call me slut, and whore, and things profane,
paint me as deadlier than their true foes.
To such as think that way, I would request
you ask yourself how feeble Tristan is,
and whether you are so keen to suggest
that King Mark could be done in with a kiss?
How fragile masculinity can be,
when men judge men through such misogyny.

IV

Mark

It's true that many say I am betrayed—
my best knight and my wife, behind my back—
but, caution to all: how a thing's portrayed
can (despite evidence's lack) persuade
us to perceive things as they never were;
and love for friends and lords, cloud judgment clear
till innocents are guilty and interred
not for what's done, but for unfounded fears
of what might have transpired. With that in mind,
let's leave these accusations where they are,
that time and space enough may let us find
the truth of Tristan, Isolde, and King Mark.
Though many men have deemed me most unwise,
I do know suspicion is how love dies.

V

Merlin

I warned him not to marry Guinevere
not to let young Mordred come of age
to keep his enemies away from here
rather than seek to be on the same page.
But Arthur does what Arthur wills to do
and I am advisor merely in name.
This king is an idealist through and through,
impossible to curb though he seem tame.
All my counsel is fallen on deaf ears,
though not for spite or ignorance ignored—
No, 'tis simply this: until a king fears
that what he's built might vanish, he is Lord.
And this is how our fair Camelot falls—
Its king invites its end into its walls.

VI

Morgan le Fay

Though Arthur be my brother, we're not friends.
Though we share genes, we've never been as one.
And for my part, I tire of amends
Demanded of me by my father's son.
It's true that I've acquired skills in magic,
And made a name for myself as "le Fay,"
And I confess that I do find it tragic
How he insists on having his own way
Regardless of the rightness of a thing,
Regardless of what it might cost his men,
Regardless of the losses it might bring,
And heedless of the warnings he's been giv'n.
Though of we two I'm deemed the one to fear,
The deadlier of this duo's Brother Dear.

VII

Arthur

It isn't all that easy, being king.
The duties of this role lie heavily
On me; that I am he to whom all bring
Their cares, their fears, their woes, so readily
Sure I can offer them succor, give all
Fair hearing and the justice that they seek.
I am he who most wishes for peaceful
Outcomes leading comitatus to the peak
Of prowess in times of war, hopeful of
Safe returns to families and farms for
The men in my charge, for whom I bear love
As great as is my love for Guinevere.
Yet, for all my good will, I often find
This world requires hardened heart and mind.

VIII

Palamedes

What does it say of me, that the two men
with whom I'm most associated are
at once both knights renowned for acumen
and also known as traitors wide and far?
I am not guilty of adultery;
have never gone behind my liege lord's back:
In fact, the greatest flaw assigned to me
is that I am a Saracen, and black
of skin; and in the end, who is to say
that these things be flaws rather than delights,
when all else about me earns highest praise,
I rank among the greatest living knights?
So, flawed and human we three well may be,
but certainly, least flawed of we be me.

IX

Balin and Balan

It's hard to be both sibling and a knight;
the rivalry both personal and pro
fessional can be too much with us, nights
lying awake, tossing to and fro,
wondering how far is too far to go
where it comes to our brotherly contests.
Our efforts to excel oft come to blows
construable as envy, not honor-
seeking—but in the end, does it matter
whether Sir Balin or Sir Balan wins
this or that joust, if the deadly splatter
of one or the other's blood means no kin
will be there to congratulate the feat?
Far better we refrain, remain complete.

X

Galahad

I am the Grail knight, pearl of matchless price
among men, God's chosen champion; yet,
while I admit the praise and honor's nice,
I despair that my deeds do not beget
similar holiness in the other knights
of the Round Table. When I joined this band
of brothers, I believed that was the height
of human achievement, yet now understand
appearances deceive; and that these men,
though brave and strong and wielding good intent
yet mortal are, with all the flaws of men,
The laws have broken and the rules have bent.
A holy knight's so out of place on Earth
it begs the question: what is knighthood worth?

XI

Gawain

Before Lancelot came along I was
everyone's favorite; but ever since
he came to court (at the queen's wish) the buzz
has been about his greatness, what a prince
he is among men. Well, I don't deny
he's a capable swordsman and peerless
on horseback; yet for all that, it is I
excel on quests, in battles am fearless.
One thing more distinguishes me from
him: I've never slept with my uncle's wife,
never forced our king to overcome
such deep betrayal and personal strife.
For all my faults (and my faults many are)
at least I know my work's not love, but war.

XII

Lancelot

I didn't even want to come to court,
but sense of duty beat out common sense,
and when our Lady begged me to report,
'twas clear that Fate had taken from my hands
the reins of my fortunes; well, so be it.
My conscience is clear; I have only done
what I've been bid to do, and if I fit
the role of villain for some, for the one
I serve I am Love, for the other,
"Most Likely to Lay Down His Life for Him,"
and this must be enough. I prefer to
die knowing I fulfilled, however grim,
the destiny God set aside for me —
so let the gossips gossip gleefully.

XIII

Guinevere

The truth is I don't think that Arthur knew
my heart or mind at all when he proposed
we marry; nor did he seek to construe
my view of the thing, he simply supposed
I'd want to be queen over all this land,
that such ambition fuels all women's hearts
and thus, I'd be delighted 'twas my hand
he chose from all the lovely women's parts
available to him as king. Poor man.
He suffers from the power that he wields—
A power that fits him to rule a land,
but not a heart. And so, his power yields
him a marriage, but not a love; for that,
I had to go and find my Lancelot.

XIV

Mordred

For God's sake, you'd think a king capable
of creating a comitatus so
renowned and seeming unassailable
could understand that anyone's a foe
who threatens that brotherhood's well-being.
And yet, here's Arthur, refusing to see
with his reason instead of his feelings
that his wife and his right-hand man must be
brought to trial, punished sans regret.
Our hale and hearty king has failed to live
up to expectation and the laws he set,
chooses over order betrayers to give
his clemency and heart—when all's said and done,
does anyone know who anyone is?

Syllables in Love

Guinevere lies in bed and thinks in syllables
with a heavy man's thigh draped across her.
Lan-ce-lot and *Gui-ne-vere* — a pair of trinities
Three syllables equal two people in love with each other
and each in love again with another
who is folded into the third syllable every time:
Lancelot is *Lan*-Lancelot and *Ce*-Guinevere and *Lot*-Arthur
and *Guinevere* is *Gui*-Guinevere and *Ne*-Lancelot and *Vere*-Arthur
and then things break down with Arthur, only they don't have to
she thinks, as she listens to the man's placid snores
and gazes at the moonlight-glowing alabaster thigh.
Because Arthur, two syllables, can be three if he is brought in as
the third, in a completion generated by embodiment of the real
and not by the possessive barriers now keeping them apart;
Not *Arthur's* Guinevere and Lancelot, which divides
But *Arthur is* Guinevere and Lancelot, which bonds
All three together in hypostasis, three-in-one
Arthur the king, Guinevere the queen, Lancelot the knight
Become Arthur the king, Arthur the queen, Arthur the knight
Or, rendered more whole still: *Arthur-king, Arthur-queen, Arthur-knight*
Or, mingled wholly, Arthur king/queen/knight transfigures:
Arthur is, *Arthuris* ...
and there are his three syllables.

And this is become now a trio of trinities:
Arthuris, Lancelot, Guinevere, all loving each other
Arthuris is *Ar*-Arthur and *Thur*-Lancelot and *Is*-Guinevere, and
Lancelot is *Lan*-Lancelot and *Ce*-Guinevere and *Lot*-Arthur, and
Guinevere is *Gui*-Guinevere and *Ne*-Lancelot and *Vere*-Arthur
Broken down and recombined, they are inextricable one from the
other:
Lan-Gui-Ar, Ce-Ne-Thur, Lot-Vere-Is,
and in this manner, love is perfectly squared away,
the lovers fully intermingled, three people in love with one love
syllabic union, love-language alchemy.

Lancelot and Guinevere Endeavor Rapprochement (Two Epistles)

Lancelot, to Guinevere:

I have generated life
and I have snuffed out life
and I have been Godlike.
And I have been an awful being
awesome in my awfulness—the Flower of Chivalry, and the
Face of *fin'amor*, and the
Father of Galahad the Grail Knight and the
Bane of Camelot.
Said and done wonderful and terrible things,
acted on basest and most honorable impulses,
gone mad in my passions and never quite recovered.
Served you both in honor and pride, and rejoiced, and cried,
felt and understood so much and nothing at all,
wanted the best and worst for myself—
And for him—
And for you.

Guinevere, to Lancelot:

I have never given birth
to anyone but you—
lover, knight-son, I brought you to Camelot,
presented my husband the king with a man

he'd be proud to call "Son"
presented my husband the king with a man
he'd be proud to call "Knight"
presented my husband the king with a man
he'd be proud to have by his side as much as me.
They whisper of us as a vexed and vexing trinity
and I say that we are, in all the ways that God and man alike, allow:
husband-wife-child
father-mother-son
king-queen-knight
lord-lady-lover
cuckold-slut-paramour
and am I so terrible, then, for loving you
as much as him?

Arthur's Choice

Do not ask me why I
choose to turn a blind eye, why
I choose them over my reign; it's
only that a man may be a king and
a king, a man, and yet
they are separate things.
And while some perform the alchemy
that transfigures the two into one:
Kingman, Manking,
single, sovereign entity,
I have never achieved this.
I know what ought to happen,
I know what should be done,
But and I do it, I am undone.
It is so, that the king should cry "Treason!"
and have both their heads—
But his, I need in battle,
and hers, I need in bed.
And the man should shout "Dishonor!"
and seek their demise—
But he is knight and brother,
and she has binding eyes.
And so, I must look away,
and Camelot will fall,
because I the king can't lose

the knight I love best of all,
and I the man must choose
the woman who enthralls.
You who read this, and disagree:
Understand that this is not about you.

Turning Leaf

Breaking from my branch I flutter
    Turning over and over, blown to and fro
        Visible from every angle and ever kaleidescopic
           Like a knight's reputation, in the
             Hands of poets.

The Kitchen Cat Weighs in With the Last Word, Shakespeare-Style

If we beasts and objects have offended,
Know that we've no wish to mend it,
That you have simply stopped in here,
Can close this book and disappear
From Arthur's world, as in a dream,
While we remain as image and theme.
Humans, to their wills do bend
Creatures and things to desired end:
And as I am an honest Cat,
You will permit me to say that
The things and creatures in these pages
Merely wish you would re-stage us;
Try to see us with fresh eyes
And not relegate us to sidelines.
Now, pet my fur, if we be friends
And thus, this little book now ends.

Notes

"What the Kitchen Cat Thought"

Camelot is the name given to King Arthur's legendary kingdom. In the nineteenth century, Victorian and Romantic writers like Alfred, Lord Tennyson and Sir Walter Scott took the stories of Arthur and his Knights of the Round Table from their origins in medieval literature (their primary source Sir Thomas Malory's late-fifteenth-century *Le Morte Darthur: Or, The Whole Book of Arthur and His Knights of the Round Table,* an attempt to collect much of the English and French Arthurian material together in a single volume) and developed them into acts of medievalism, transforming tales that often criticized the social and political constructs of their place and time into escapist literature that reimagined the medieval period as a noble and heroic Golden Age. This idealized version of the legend is the one most familiar to modern audiences, and the one about which the kitchen cat ruminates with skepticism.

"A Cut Rose in Guinevere's Chamber Meditates on Mortality"

Guinevere is King Arthur's wife, Queen of Camelot. According to the French *Vulgate Merlin* tale cycle, she is the daughter of King Leodegrance of Cameliard, one of Arthur's father, King Uther's, allies.

"What a Chicken Noticed About Sir Kay"

Sir Kay is Arthur's foster-brother and becomes the seneschal of Camelot (the steward, or officer, of domestic responsibilities in a medieval household) when Arthur ascends to the throne as king. In most stories, Kay is presented as hot-headed, stubborn, surly, and rude, with a biting tongue and great disdain in particular for Guinevere.

"The Rain Explains Something About Arthurian Tournaments"

"Chivalry" is a deeply misunderstood concept in today's world. In the medieval world of Arthur and his knights, it was a system of rules and regulations governing knightly conduct particularly regarding battlefields, jousts, and tournaments. It is often conflated in modern understandings with "courtly love" which was essentially a conduct game developed in the court of Eleanor of Aquitaine and her daughter, Marie de Champagne, and emphasized relationships between lords and ladies.

"Mother Moon Beams Down on Her Favorite"

Sir Galahad is the (illegitimate) son of Sir Lancelot. Raised by nuns, he eventually comes to Camelot where he fulfills the prophecy of the Siege Perilous ("Perilous Seat"). The siege perilous is a vacant seat at the Round Table that can only be filled by "the best knight of the world." Galahad proves himself to be the seat's rightful claimant by pulling a sword from a stone in the middle of a river, and this event sets into motion the famous Quest for the Holy Grail, which Galahad achieves (together with Sir Perceval and Sir Bors).

"A Sheep Sets Things Straight Concerning Castle-Field Relations"

One of the prevailing themes throughout medieval Arthurian

narratives, especially those from the French and Anglo-Norman traditions, is secrecy. Secrets—who has them, who keeps them, who uses them against who—are often essential elements in Arthurian stories, such as the *lais* of Marie de France, and this poem pays homage to that tradition.

"The Wishing Well Wishes"

The wishing well is a product of European folklore, stemming from the belief that water houses deities and sacred spaces where water was kept could become places where such deities might be summoned through rituals, including offering gifts to the deities such as coins. As far as I know there is not actually a wishing well in Arthurian stories, although bodies of water more generally play prominent roles.

"The Wishing Well Dishes"

Sir Pellinore appears prominently in the 13th century French Post-Vulgate Arthurian story cycle and also in Malory's *Morte Darthur* (and more recently and perhaps, endearingly, in T.H. White's *Once and Future King* and its 1963 Disney animated film adaptation, *The Sword in the Stone*). He is presented always as being on an endless hunt of the Questing Beast (See: note for "The Questing Beast Joins #MeToo.") Palamedes is a Saracen (Muslim) knight, traditionally the son of the King of Babylon (present-day Iraq), who joins Arthur's Round Table, appearing in the *Prose Tristan* cycle of French stories and from there, making his way into the pages of Malory's *Morte Darthur*. He is a rival of Tristan's for the love of La Belle Iseult (Isolde the Fair.) Sir Gareth and Sir Gaheris are two of Sir Gawain's brothers; all together with their fourth brother, Sir Agravaine, they are known as the Orkney brothers and, in Malory, they are highly clannish and prone to violent retribution against their enemies, even killing their mother for a perceived slight on the family honor. Gareth and Gaheris are killed during the raid to arrest Lancelot and Guinevere in the climactic chapter of the *Morte Darthur*, plunging the kingdom into its downfall when Gawain refuses to accept Lancelot's apology for his brothers' deaths. Gareth's death here is particularly tragic, as he is beloved of Sir Lancelot, who blames himself for Gareth's death, among other things.

"A Sword in the Armory"

Bronze horseshoes have been found in Etruscan tombs from the 5th century BCE and appear regularly in excavations of early medieval sites throughout Europe. The first evidence of iron horseshoes is documented at the 10th century CE (although this may not be their origin, since iron was such a precious commodity that it's probable that used horseshoes would be melted down and turned into something else.) By the 13th and 14th centuries, when Arthurian legends were flowering throughout Europe, iron horseshoes were in regular use. Swords made of iron first appear in the Iron Age (approximately the 12th century BCE) and become widespread by the 8th century CE.

"The Questing Beast Joins #MeToo"

The Questing Beast is variously associated with Sir Pellinore, Sir Percival, and Sir Palamedes, most often and most notably with Sir Pellinore. Described as having the head and neck of a snake, a leopard's body, a lion's hindquarters, and rabbit's feet, it is distinguished as well by a barking noise like that of a fox which it emits from its belly. Typically ungendered in its presentation, I have elected to assign it female gender (with linguistic support, since in French, the language in which tales featuring this creature originated, the word "beast," or "bête" is gendered feminine) for the purposes of this poem.

"A Sheet's Analysis of What Goes on Between the Sheets"

The inspection of bedding following a wedding-night to ascertain whether or not the woman was a virgin by dint of the presence (or lack thereof) of the blood that indicates a broken hymen is a tradition linked to the concept of primogeniture—the eldest son of a family inheriting the family's fortunes—and thus, the need to ensure that any child that resulted from the union of a man and woman was, in fact, the man's, only believed to be definite if the woman were a virgin at the time of inception. This practice is documented at least as far back as the medieval period. As many of Arthur's knights, Arthur, himself, and his wife, engage in extramarital sexual affairs, some of these resulting in important figures (among these, King Arthur and the Grail Knights Galahad and Percival) and many of them, instances of rape, this idea of a woman's honor being tied to her virginity and that virginity, being essential in turn to a man's honor and legitimacy, is fraught and problematic in medieval stories, and continues to be fraught and problematic in today's society.

"The Great Hall"

Throughout the medieval period, central halls featured prominently in European communities, and the feast hall is an essential element of many of the most famous European medieval texts, including *Beowulf, Sir Gawain and the Green Knight,* and the *Nibelungenlied.* In literature, the feast hall, or great hall, is frequently the site both of festive celebrations and of violent altercations.

"A Lyre Begs a Commission"

European lyres developed in the early medieval period (beginning around c. 7th century CE), came in several variations of size and style, could include or not include a fingerboard, and were frequently played with a bow. While the Anglo-Saxon hearpe was in fact a lyre, it gave its name ("hearpe") to a different stringed instrument, the harp. However, lutes and harps are not the same instrument. Morgan le Fay is King Arthur's half-sister, variously portrayed as a sorceress, a goddess, and a fairy; associated with necromancy and with the Isle of Avalon, and typically presented as an antagonist of Camelot, particularly of Guinevere.

"The Lyre's Limericks, I"

Limericks were invented as a generally comic poetic form in the eighteenth century and popularized in England in the nineteenth century. They are not typically associated with the Arthurian legend. Lancelot du Lac ("Lancelot of the Lake") is the French title for Sir Lancelot, who in that tradition is raised by the Lady of the Lake. Lord Bertilak, and Bertilak's Lady, are featured characters in *Sir Gawain and the Green Knight*, in which they appear as Morgan le Fay's instruments in an elaborate scheme to frighten Queen Guinevere to death.

"The Rosary of the Hermit in the Wood Reminds You of the Importance of Faith and Hope in Stories"

Modern audiences may find it strange that I include hermits, friars, nuns, and similar religious figures in this collection of poems, but in fact such characters play important roles throughout the Arthurian legend; Galahad, for instance, is raised by nuns, and Lancelot spends time in the forest with a hermit. They often appear at key moments, bringing important ethical and moral considerations to bear on the events of individual knights' stories.

"A Ring in the Treasury Summarizes the Basic Arthurian Tale Plot"

The *bel inconnu* (French for "Fair Unknown") is one of the essential motifs in the Arthurian legend. The original *bel inconnu* is Sir Gingalain, who ultimately proves himself to be Sir Gawain's son. Other Fair Unknown figures include Galahad, Perceval, and Gareth. Female Fair Unknown tales include that of Silence and Melusine.

"Gawain's Shield Admires Her Pentagram Tattoo"

In *Sir Gawain and the Green Knight*, Sir Gawain is armed with a shield that has the Virgin Mary's face on one side, and on the other a pentagram, or pentangle, signifying Gawain's perfection: his five perfect senses, the five perfect fingers on his hand, his faithfulness to the five wounds of Christ, his conviction in the five joys Mary, Mother of Jesus has in Christ, and his exemplary embodiment of the five virtues of knighthood fellowship, generosity, chastity, charity, and courtesy, which not uncoincidentally are also key virtues of medieval Christianity.)

"The Door to Guinevere's Bedchamber Resigns"

This poem deals with the subject of treason, which is essential in the Arthurian legend, particularly in those tales that developed during and following the English Wars of the Roses, which led to a heightened and widespread anxiety over treachery in all its forms.

"A Goose Feather Quill Refuses to Spill Secrets"

Goose feathers—especially from the left wing, for right-handed writers, and usually only the first 6 of the feathers on the wing—were the preferred writing implement of medieval scribes. More costly swan feather quills could be used for larger lettering, such as the illuminated letters in luxury manuscripts, crow feathers were frequently employed for business writing, such as account-ledgers, and eagle, owl, and hawk feathers (and in America, turkey) could also be employed.

"The Cat with her Basket of Kittens in the Scullery I"

This poem deals with the central tragedy of the essential Arthurian legend, which is that Queen Guinevere never gives birth to an heir to the kingdom, so that when Arthur falls in battle, Camelot and the Knights of the Round Table dissolve as a community. There are variations on this matter, but they are rare. In some stories (the French *Lanzelet* and *Perlesvaus* and German *Parzeval*) they have a son, Loholt, who is variously killed by Sir Kay or dies of illness. In the Latin *Historia Brittonum* ("History of Britain") of the 9th century, and in the slightly later Welsh prose romance *Geraint*, Arthur has a son, Amhar, whose origins are not explained; in the former Arthur kills and buries his son, himself, with no explanation given. Still in the Welsh tradition, Arthur also has a son, Gwydre, who is killed on a boar hunt in the romance *Culhwch and Olwen*, and sons listed in the triads— short historical bardic texts—but again, no explanation of their birth or what happens to them is given. Mordred, of course, is also Arthur's son, product of an incestuous affair with his sister, Morgause. In the *Alliterative Morte Arthure*, Guinevere is taken to wife by Mordred in Arthur's absence, and they have two sons, whom Arthur orders killed (in the earlier *Historia Regum Brittaniae* ["History of the Kings of Britain"] of Geoffrey of Monmouth, Arthur also orders Mordred and his sons killed; but Mordred is not yet described as Arthur's son.) In none of these stories do Arthur's children outlive him; any such tale is a modern development.

"The Cat with her Basket of Kittens in the Scullery II"

King Arthur demonstrates a proclivity for testing his knights with these sorts of competitions, which then morph into quests: early on in Malory's *Morte Darthur*, he has them try to pull a sword from a scabbard, which jumpstarts the story of Balin and Balan; later, they try to pull a sword from a stone to determine who is the best knight in the world—and, of course, Arthur himself gains his throne through a similar trial.

"Arthurian Ants Join the Unionization Effort"

This poem is the first of several to mention the central incident in the tale of Sir Mador de la Porte, a scene in several of the "Death of Arthur" narratives. After Guinevere banishes Lancelot from court for his infidelity towards her, she throws a feast to demonstrate to the other knights that she loves them as much as him. During this feast, a knight is killed by a poisoned apple that has been slipped into a basket of fruit on the table, which leads to Guinevere's being accused of murder, the inciting incident for Lancelot's return to court and the ultimate downfall of Camelot.

"The Lyre and a Harp Compose a Jumping-Rope Ditty for Arthurian Dude-Bros"

This ditty is based on the popular jump-rope song "Miss Mary Mack-Mack-Mack." Here, the subject matter is Lady Bertilak, the wife of Lord Bertilak, an important character in the popular Middle English romance *Sir Gawain and the Green Knight*. Lady Bertilak's role is that of temptress; while her husband is out hunting, she sneaks into Gawain's room and tries to get him to have sex with her. Gawain manages (for the most part) to avoid this by pretending to be asleep. This poem is critical of "bro" culture, in which it is expected that a man in that position would, obviously, sleep with the woman. The situation in *Sir Gawain and the Green Knight* is actually unusual, as typically Gawain is well-known for his "sexcapades."

"What a Poet Writes of Excalibur"

This poem references "The Once and Future King" (*Rex quondam, rexque futurus*), which is the motto assigned to King Arthur by Geoffrey of Monmouth, his first biographer, who writes that when Arthur is mortally wounded in battle, he is taken to the Isle of Avalon to have his wounds tended by the magical women who live there, and that as Once and Future King, one day he will return when England has need of him. In the English tradition, Excalibur is given to Arthur by the Lady of the Lake and through her can be tied, however tenuously, to Avalon. The lines "Romance will lose luster / and war win out" refers to the dwindling popularity of romance narratives at the end of the medieval period, and the rising interest, for instance by the Tudor dynasty, in connecting themselves to the Arthurian legend historically as a means of validating their right to rule.

"Excalibur Deals with Imposter Syndrome"

In the English tradition, Arthur's sword in the stone is not the same sword as Excalibur, which is later given to him by the Lady of the Lake (in the French tradition, this distinction is not made.) In English versions, the sword in the stone is located in an anvil on top of a stone in a churchyard, labeled with the statement: "Whoso pulleth out this sword from the stone and anvil is rightwise king born of all England." Arthur, serving as the squire to newly-knighted Sir Kay, pulls it out secretly when Kay has forgotten his sword and needs one for a tournament. His foster-father, Sir Ector, and Kay recognize the sword and ask where he got it. Arthur then repeats his actions in front of a crowd of witnesses to show that he did, indeed, pull the sword, thus winning the right to be king. Excalibur serves as a symbol of Arthur's sovereignty, but in most stories it is the scabbard that possesses magical powers, preventing the death of its wearer regardless of how much blood is lost (in some versions, preventing bleeding at all.) The scabbard's magic is not a secret; Morgan le Fay steals it to try to put

Arthur in peril. *Caledfwlch* is the Welsh name for Arthur's sword, appearing in *Culhwch and Olwen*.

"The Poisoned Apple's Unrecorded Testimony"

This is the second poem in this collection dealing with the poisoned apple at Guinevere's feast in the tale of Sir Mador de la Porte (See: note for "Arthurian Ants Join the Unionization Effort.") While the poisoned apple scene appears in multiple narratives, including the French *Roi le Mort Artu* and the English *Stanzaic Morte Arthure*, this poem is based on Malory's version of the events, which is the only medieval Death of Arthur narrative to assign the poisoned knight a name, "Sir Patryse"; in the earlier texts, he is simply referred to as "the Scottish knight." Sir Pyonell poisons the apple because he expects Sir Gawain to eat it; he seeks revenge on Sir Gawain for killing one of Pyonell's kinsmen, Sir Lamorak, who was Sir Gawain's mother's illicit lover, killed when the Orkney brothers surprised them together in bed and decided their mother must pay for dishonoring the family in that way. Sir Gawain is expected to eat the apple because he is traditionally associated with loving fruit and eating it at every meal.

"The Round Table Doesn't Get It"

Traditionally, the Round Table is a gift to Arthur upon his marriage to Guinevere from his new father-in-law, Guinevere's father Sir Leodegrance. It was designed to have no head, so that everyone who sat at it was seated equally, in comparison to more traditional Hall furnishings, where a table at a high dais set above all others was where the members of a community deemed (or who deemed themselves) most important would sit, with everyone else seated in proximity to that table according to rank and privilege; a seating arrangement that continues to be employed at many modern Western European and American events, including weddings and State

Dinners. The Round Table, by contrast, was meant to erase the hierarchy, forging instead an alliance of equal shareholders in the community, with no man seated over another.

"Hairs in a Horn Comb"

This poem was inspired by the French prose romance "Lancelot: Or the Knight of the Cart," by Chrétien de Troyes. In that tale, among his many adventures as he seeks to rescue the stolen-away Guinevere from Sir Meleagant, Lancelot spends the night in a castle whose maiden seeks to seduce him. The next morning, she and many of her retinue accompany him on his travels. They come across a golden and ivory comb with golden hairs in it lying on a stone in the middle of a meadow. Lancelot removes the hairs from the comb for himself and gives the comb to the lady.

"Hey, Nonny Nonny"

This ditty is built off of the refrain for the song "Sigh No More" in William Shakespeare's *Much Ado About Nothing* (Act 2, scene iii)

"The Grail"

The *Quest for the Holy Grail* is one of the centerpieces of the Arthurian legend, first appearing in Robert de Boron's 13th century French Grail cycle of stories. The Knights of the Round Table embark upon a quest to locate the chalice of Joseph of Arimathea, which is believed to have been the cup into which Christ's blood was collected by Joseph when he was stabbed in the side by a spear during the Crucifixion; Joseph then took the cup to Avalon, where it was guarded until the rise of Arthur and the prophesied Grail Knight, Perceval. The finding, or achieving, of the Grail meant everlasting life for its finder, and the end of the Fisher King's Wasteland, signifying a renewed life and bounty in the world. Alternately, the Grail has been viewed as the cup of Christ's Last Supper, and as a vessel, representative of the Divine Feminine and thus a symbol for New Age goddess worship.

"Tristan"; "Isolde"; and "Mark"

The Tristan and Isolde narrative is another branch of the Arthurian legend, primary popular in the French and German traditions and pre-dating the Lancelot/Guinevere/Arthur stories, in the development of which Tristan and Isolde almost certainly had some influence. In the basic plot, Tristan defeats the Irish giant Morholt in a contest of arms and brings Isolde the Fair back to Cornwall for his uncle, King Mark, who wishes to marry her. On the way, they become extremely thirsty and, unaware of its nature, drink a love potion sent along with Isolde to help her fall in love with Mark. They fall deeply in love with one another, embarking upon an adulterous affair that causes all three of them deep pain and suffering.

"Palamedes"

In courtly versions of Tristan and Isolde, Palamedes falls in love with Isolde but, losing a joust against Tristan, forfeits his right to her. Tristan, of course, then embarks upon an adulterous affair with her. Palamedes also finds himself up against Lancelot in jousting, and the three of these knights typically are viewed as the best in tournaments.

"Balin and Balan"

Balin and Balan are characters in Sir Thomas Malory's *Morte Darthur*. They are twin brothers. Balin undergoes a series of unfortunate events in which he is released from prison after a six months' stay for killing one of Arthur's cousins; wins the contest to pull the sword from its scabbard and then refuses to return the sword and scabbard to the maiden who initiated the contest, resulting in the curse that he will kill the one he loves best in this world and himself be destroyed; kills the Lady of the Lake and is exiled from court for it; finds himself lost and in several violent skirmishes that lead to the untimely deaths of several maidens and, ultimately, the Dolorous Stroke, beginning the Fisher King narrative, and a deadly duel with a stranger in the woods who turns out to be his twin brother, Balan, which results in both their deaths.

"The Kitchen Cat Weighs in With the Last Word, Shakespeare-Style"

This poem is modeled on Puck's monologue in Act V, scene i of William Shakespeare's A *Midsummer Night's Dream.*

Recommended for Further Reading

It would be impossible for me to list all of the available resources for learning more about the Arthurian legend; however, readers who are interested in the Arthurian legends may enjoy the following resources as starting points:

Internet Resources

The Camelot Project, hosted by the Rochester University Robbins Library: https://d.lib.rochester.edu/camelot-project

The "Arthurian Legends" pages at *Timeless Myths*, created by Jimmy Joe: http://www.timelessmyths.com/arthurian/

Hetta Elizabeth Howes's article, "The Legends of King Arthur" hosted at the British Library online: https://www.bl.uk/medieval-literature/articles/the-legends-of-king-arthur

"Quondam et Futurus: The Once and Future Wiki about King Arthur and the Knights of the Round Table," hosted at Fandom.com: https://kingarthur.fandom.com/wiki/King_Arthur_Wiki

"King Arthur" podcasts at *Myths and Legends* by Bardic Enterprises: https://www.mythpodcast.com/tag/king-arthur/

"Best Arthurian Podcasts of 2019" hosted at Player FM: https://player.fm/podcasts/ArthurianX

Literature

Where to begin? There are thousands of Arthurian books in almost every genre imaginable. My recommendation for those who are not very familiar with Arthurian literature is to start with Sir Thomas Malory's *Le Morte Darthur* since that's more or less the foundational version of the Arthurian legend for English readers. Those who are interested in medieval Arthurian literature may also want to check out Marie de France's "Lanval" and "Chevrefoil," the famous *Sir Gawain and the Green Knight*, Béroul's "Romance of Tristan," Wolfram von Eschenbach's Parzifal, Chrétien de Troyes' "the Knight of the Cart" and "the Knight of the Lion," and, for good fun, the Old Norse "Saga of the Mantle." The English Renaissance epic poem *The Faerie Queene*, by Sir Edmund Spenser, is absolutely delightful, although if you are not comfortable reading Renaissance English (think Shakespeare) it might be tricky at first. If you are interested in poetry, there's the *Idylls of the King*, by Alfred, Lord Tennyson; *The Waste-Land*, by T.S. Eliot; Margaret Atwood's "Avalon Revisited," and Margaret Lloyd's *A Moment in the Field: Voices From the Arthurian Legend*, for starters. More modern prose literary works featuring the Arthurian legends include Mark Twain's time-travel novel *A Connecticut Yankee in King Arthur's Court*; T.H. White's wonderful *The Once and Future King*, Marion Zimmerman Bradley's *Mists of Avalon,* and Phyllis Ann Carr's murder mystery *Idylls of the Queen*. Meg Cabot's young adult novel *Avalon High*, Alessa Eleffson's *Blood of the Fey*, and Katherine Sparrow's *Fay Morgan Chronicles* are good starts for readers interested in writers that reimagine the Arthurian legend in modern settings with modern characters. Readers interested in fiction about Merlin can check out Mary Stewart's Merlin trilogy (*The Crystal Cave, The Hollow Hills,* and *The Last Enchantment*), Jane Yolen's *Merlin's Booke,* or T.A. Barron's *Lost Merlin* series; readers interested in Morgan le Fay can try Nancy Springer's *I am Morgan le Fay* or Lavinia Collins's *Morgan: An Arthurian Fantasy*. Readers who like Sir Gawain can check out Gillian Bradshaw's *Hawk of May*. Lancelot lovers may enjoy Giles Christian's *Lancelot,* and those fascinated by Guinevere might check out Sharan Newman's *Guinevere,* Nancy McKenzie's *Queen of Camelot,* or Alice Borshardt's *Tales of Guinevere*. More Tristan and Isolde can be found in Rosalind Miles's trilogy (*Isolde, Queen of the Western Isle; The Maid of the White Hands;* and *The Lady of the Sea.*) Science fiction enthusiasts may enjoy Andre Norton's *Merlin's Mirror, Camelot 3000,* Patricia Keneally-Morrison's *Keltiad,* or C. J. Cherryh's *Port Eternity,* or you may want to check out Amy Rose Capetta and Cori McCarthy's queer Arthurian space opera, *Once and Future*. If you didn't see anything in this list that caught your attention, feel free to drop me a line—I have plenty more suggestions!

About the Author

Melissa Ridley Elmes is a lifelong, laminated card-carrying member of the geek club, which means she was nerdy before it became a trendy thing to be. In addition to her obsession with the Arthurian legends in all their permutations, she is fascinated by mythology and folklore from around the world, languages, worldbuilding, medieval literature and culture and their modern adaptations, and dragons. Her Day Job is Assistant Professor of English, which means she figured out how to get paid to read books and talk about them. She (currently) enjoys tabletop RPGs, *Skyrim*, and *Horizon Zero Dawn*, a list subject to change without notice, and her new pipe dream (having finished this book) is to score an invitation to play Dungeons and Dragons with the cast of *Critical Role* and to invent a nerdy mixed drink for Brian Foster to test on *Between the Sheets*.

About the Illustrator

Anna Elmes grew up reading a lot of fantasy novels and surrounded by art. She started drawing seriously in the 5th grade, when she and some of her friends began writing stories and creating characters together. Ever since, she's been learning new skills and growing as an artist. Much of her inspiration comes from the books that she reads and animated television shows like *Steven Universe, Star vs the Forces of Evil, Phineas and Ferb*, and *She-Ra: Princesses of Power*. During the day, she's a 10th grade high school student taking as many classes as she can possibly cram into her schedule. She loves creating stories, designing characters, tabletop roleplaying games, and *The Adventure Zone* podcast (which she insists is better than *Critical Role*).

CPSIA information can be obtained
at www.ICGtesting.com
Printed in the USA
LVHW040020200722
723927LV00014B/120